To my nephew and his footie mad dad

MYRIAD BOOKS LIMITED
35 Bishopsthorpe Road, London SE26 4PA

First published in 2003 by
PICCADILLY PRESS LIMITED
5 Castle Road, London NW1 8PR
www.piccadillypress.co.uk

ISBN 1 905606 74 5

Printed in China

Wilbie
Footie
Mad!

Sally
Chambers

MYRIAD BOOKS LIMITED

Wilbie was a duck with a passion.
A passion for football.

When Wilbie was small, his dad watched football
all the time. So Wilbie watched it too.

And now Wilbie was bigger, he was football mad!

He collected as much as he could about football.

He read as much as he could about football.

He watched as much as he could about football.

And he listened to as many stories as he could about football.

And sometimes, if he was really lucky, his dad would take him to see his favourite team play.

In fact, Wilbie had watched and collected and read and listened to so much about football that he felt sure he must be brilliant at *playing* football.

He decided to show everyone how good he was by trying out for the team.

Wilbie waited with
excitement until it was
his turn to show off
his skills.

But he hardly managed to dribble the ball . . .

He missed the ball completely when he was supposed to be heading it . . .

He tried to keep the ball in the air, but it kept hitting him on the head.

When his turn was over, Wilbie knew he was terrible at football and that he wasn't going to make the team.

But the coach could see how keen Wilbie was.

"We do need someone to do important jobs like carrying the balls and fetching the half-time oranges," he said as Wilbie was about to leave with his dad. "Perhaps you would like to help us out."

Wilbie nodded. But he felt very sad on the way home. "Never mind, son," said his dad. "You don't have to be the best — it's enjoying yourself that counts. If we practise, I'm sure you will get better."

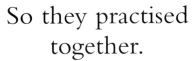

So they practised
together.

They dribbled
and jogged.

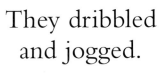

They headed
and hugged.

They scored goals
and they saved goals.

And they laughed a lot
of the time.

Wilbie loved being
with his dad.

Every Saturday, Wilbie worked really hard to help the team.

He carried and collected balls and rushed about with
the water.

He brought the oranges out at half-time.

And he cheered as loudly as he could for the team.

Then one Saturday, something exciting happened. Wilbie was waiting on the bench when the coach came to talk to him.

"The other players have decided that you have been so helpful that they'd like you to play," he said.

Wilbie was a bit
nervous at first, but
soon he was having
fun. All the practice
had helped and he was
playing well.

And then suddenly, while he was dribbling the ball up the field, he saw a chance . . . He passed it to the striker . . .

GOAL!

The final whistle blew –
Wilbie's team had won.

Everyone was cheering.
"Good passing," said the coach. "Perhaps in the future we will have a place for you in the team."

Wilbie's dad felt very proud.

On the way home, Wilbie said to his dad, "Today was great. But I don't mind if I'm not picked for the team. There is something I like better."

"What's that?" asked his dad.
"Practising with you."